DISNEP PRESENTS A PIXAR FILM

THE INCREDIBLES

RETURN OF THE SUPERS!

Adapted by Annie Auerbach
Illustrated by the Disney Storybook Artists
Designed by Tony Fejeran of Disney Publishing's Global Design Group
Inspired by the art and character designs created by Pixar Animation Studios

A Random House PICTUREBACK® Book

Random House 🏠 New York

Copyright © 2004 Disney Enterprises, Inc./Pixar Animation Studios. All rights reserved under International and Pan-American Copyright Conventions. Published in the United States by Random House Children's Books, a division of Random House, Inc., New York, and simultaneously in Canada by Random House of Canada Limited, Toronto, in conjunction with Disney Enterprises, Inc. PICTUREBACK, RANDOM HOUSE, and the Random House colophon are registered trademarks of Random House, Inc.

The term OMNIDROID used by permission of Lucasfilm Ltd.

Library of Congress Control Number: 2004093752
ISBN: 0-7364-2272-2

www.randomhouse.com/kids/disney

Printed in the United States of America
10 9 8 7 6 5 4 3

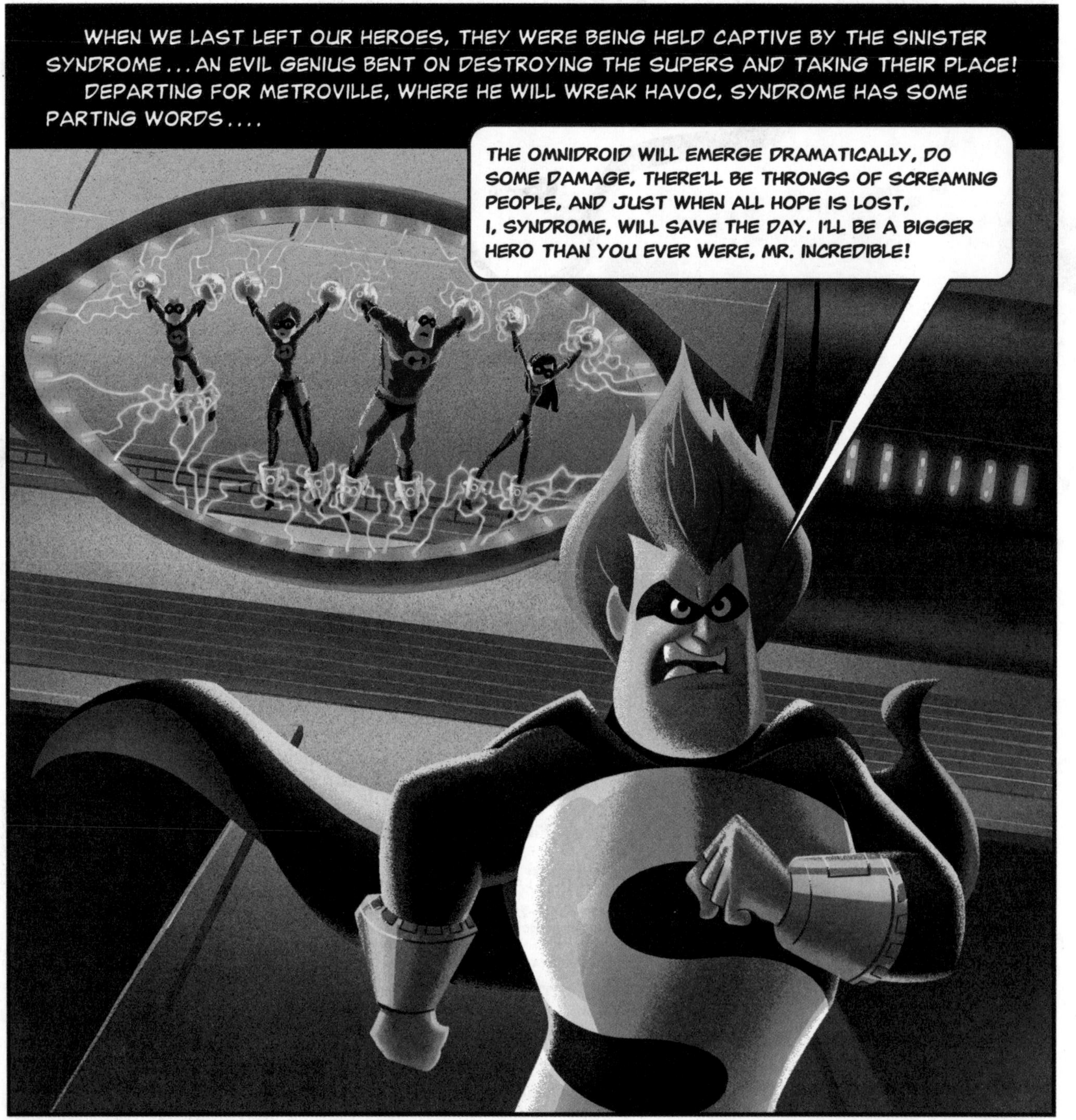
WHEN WE LAST LEFT OUR HEROES, THEY WERE BEING HELD CAPTIVE BY THE SINISTER SYNDROME . . . AN EVIL GENIUS BENT ON DESTROYING THE SUPERS AND TAKING THEIR PLACE! DEPARTING FOR METROVILLE, WHERE HE WILL WREAK HAVOC, SYNDROME HAS SOME PARTING WORDS . . . .
THE OMNIDROID WILL EMERGE DRAMATICALLY, DO SOME DAMAGE, THERE'LL BE THRONGS OF SCREAMING PEOPLE, AND JUST WHEN ALL HOPE IS LOST, I, SYNDROME, WILL SAVE THE DAY. I'LL BE A BIGGER HERO THAN YOU EVER WERE, MR. INCREDIBLE!

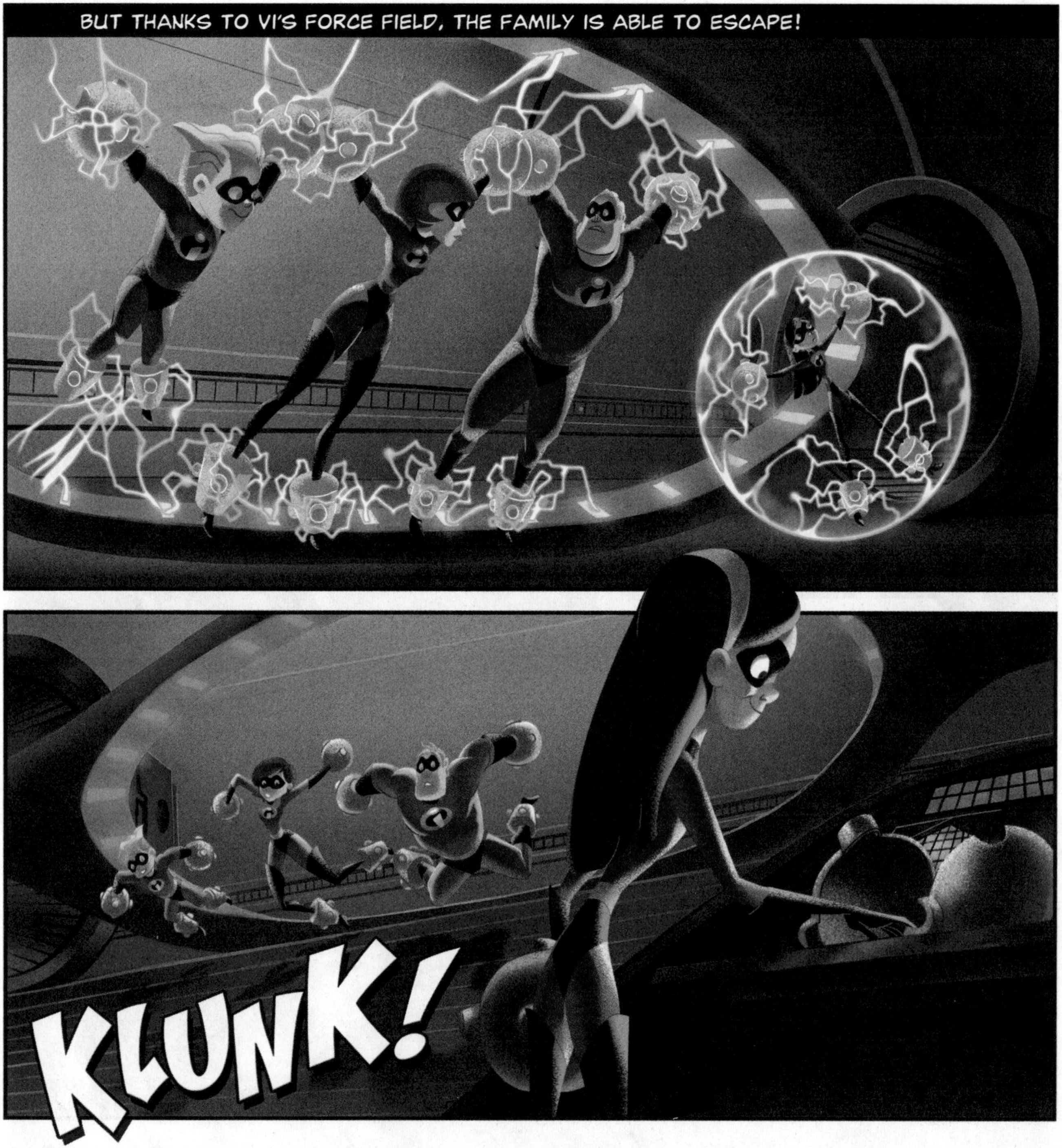
BUT THANKS TO VI'S FORCE FIELD, THE FAMILY IS ABLE TO ESCAPE!
KLUNK!

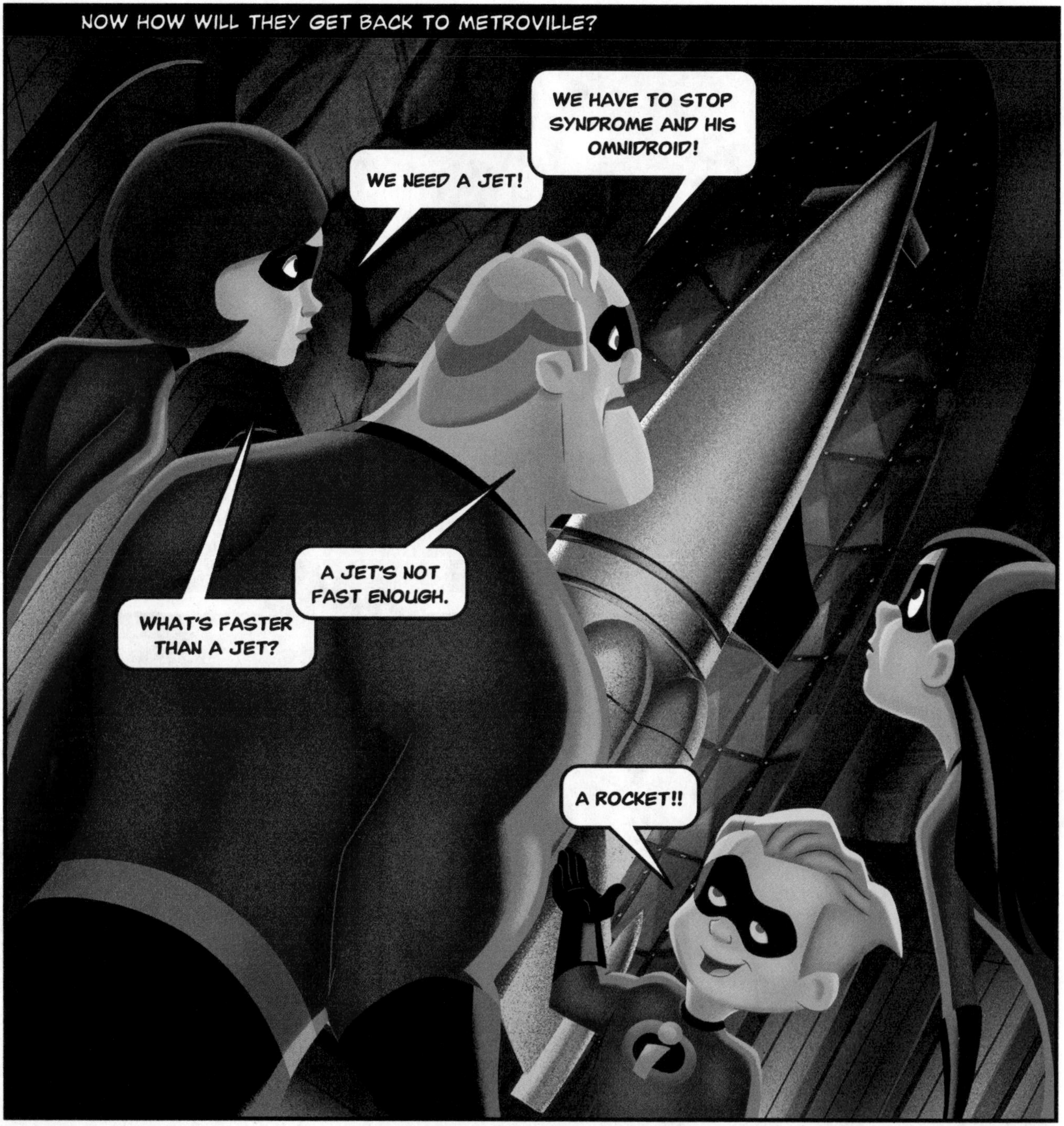
NOW HOW WILL THEY GET BACK TO METROVILLE?
WE NEED A JET!
WE HAVE TO STOP SYNDROME AND HIS OMNIDROID!
A JET'S NOT FAST ENOUGH.
WHAT'S FASTER THAN A JET?
A ROCKET!!

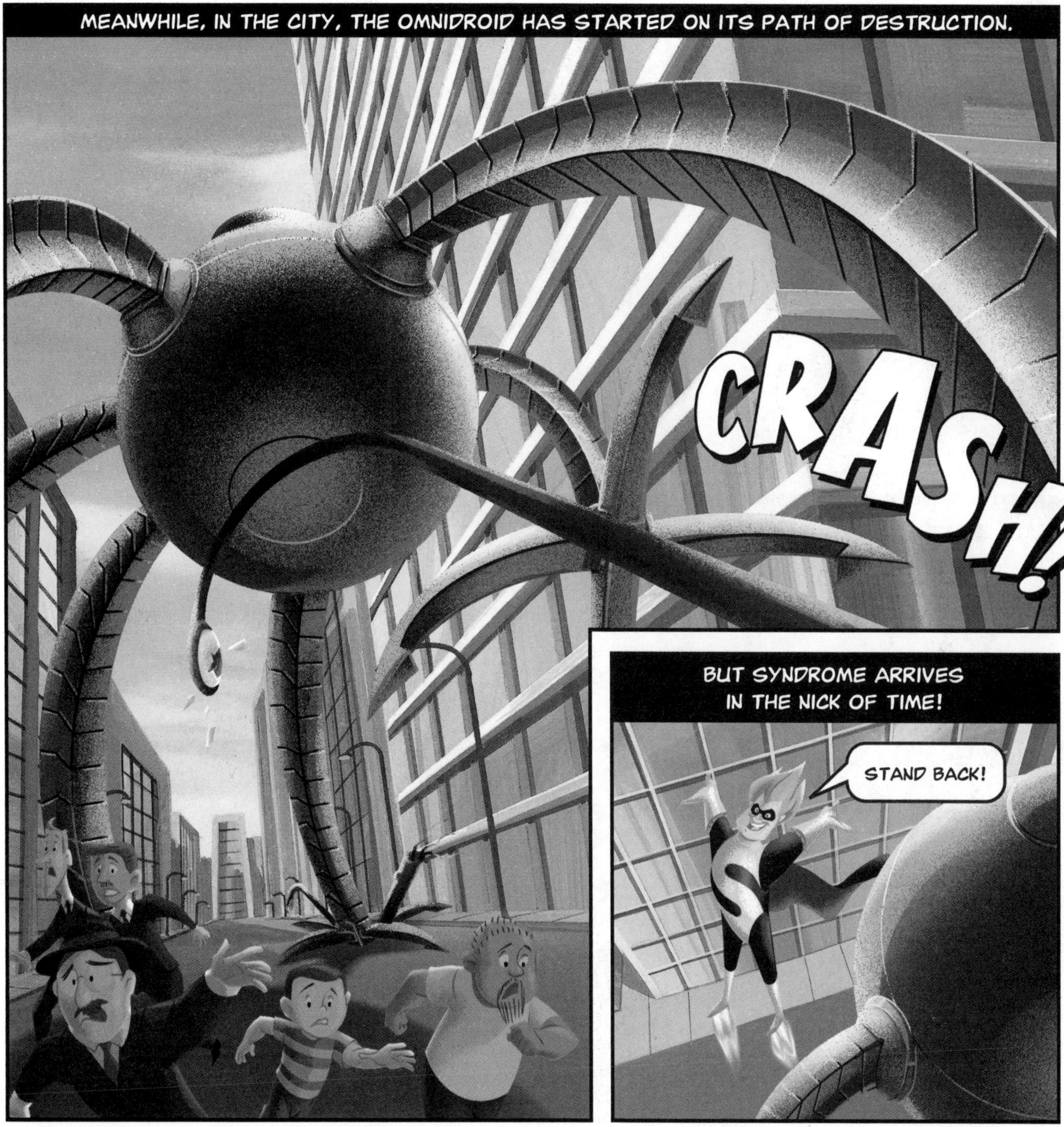
MEANWHILE, IN THE CITY, THE OMNIDROID HAS STARTED ON ITS PATH OF DESTRUCTION.
CRASH!
BUT SYNDROME ARRIVES IN THE NICK OF TIME!
STAND BACK!

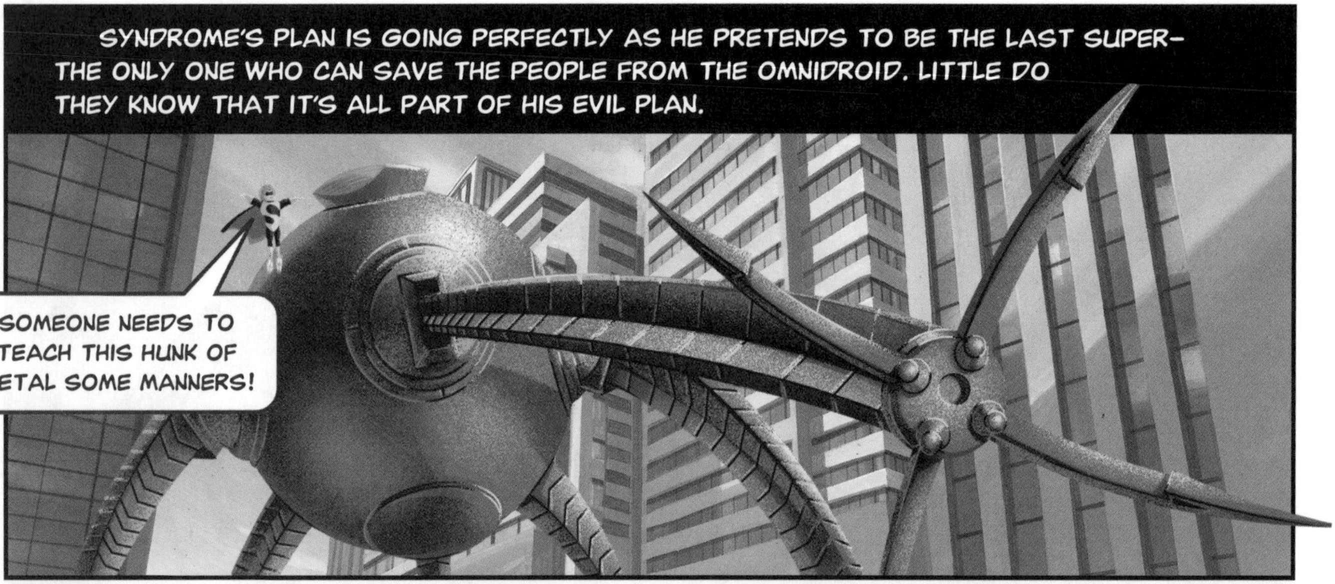
SYNDROME'S PLAN IS GOING PERFECTLY AS HE PRETENDS TO BE THE LAST SUPER–THE ONLY ONE WHO CAN SAVE THE PEOPLE FROM THE OMNIDROID. LITTLE DO THEY KNOW THAT IT'S ALL PART OF HIS EVIL PLAN.
SOMEONE NEEDS TO TEACH THIS HUNK OF METAL SOME MANNERS!

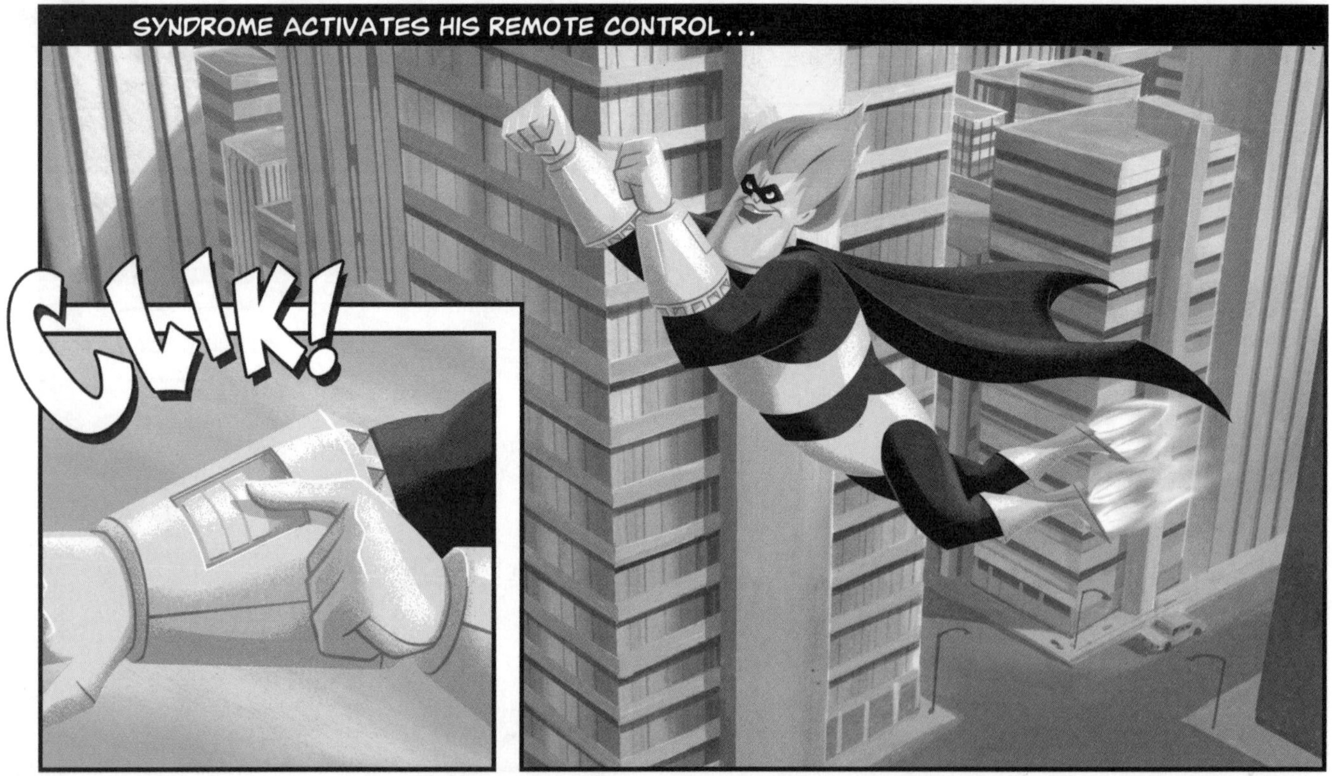
SYNDROME ACTIVATES HIS REMOTE CONTROL...
CLIK!

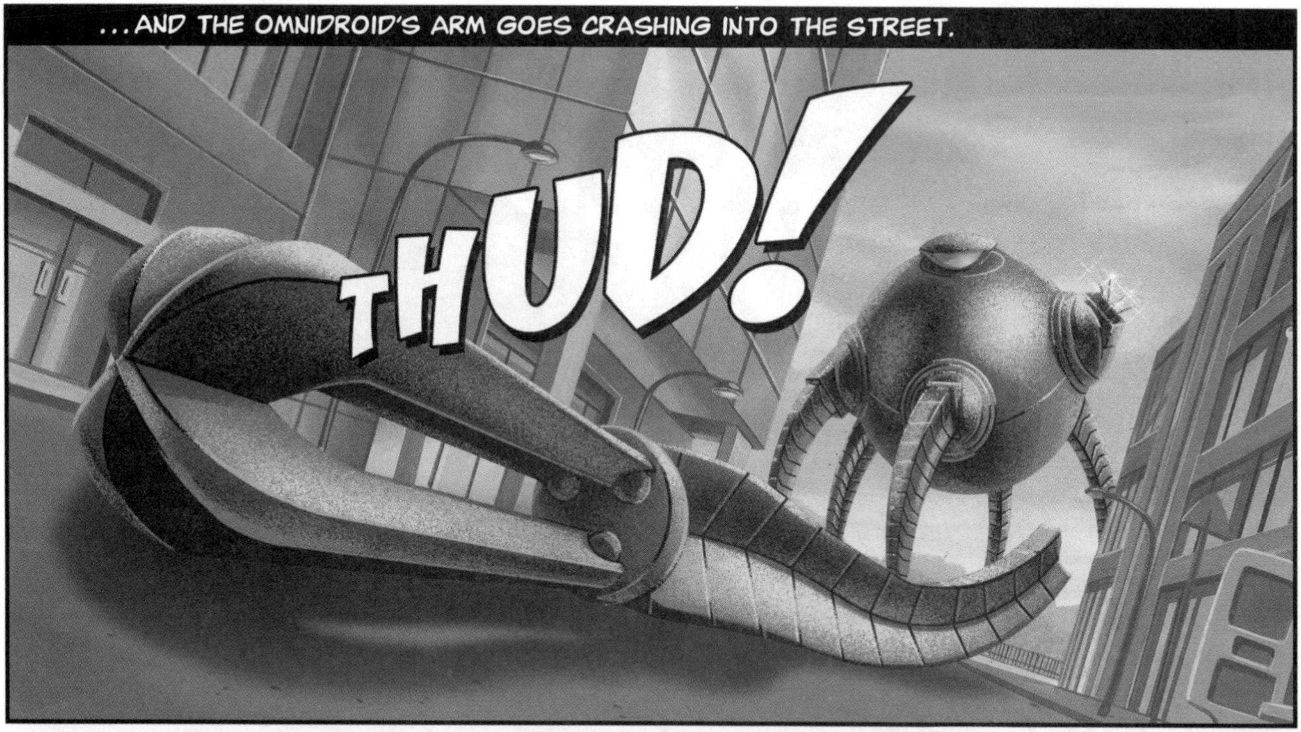
...AND THE OMNIDROID'S ARM GOES CRASHING INTO THE STREET.
THUD!

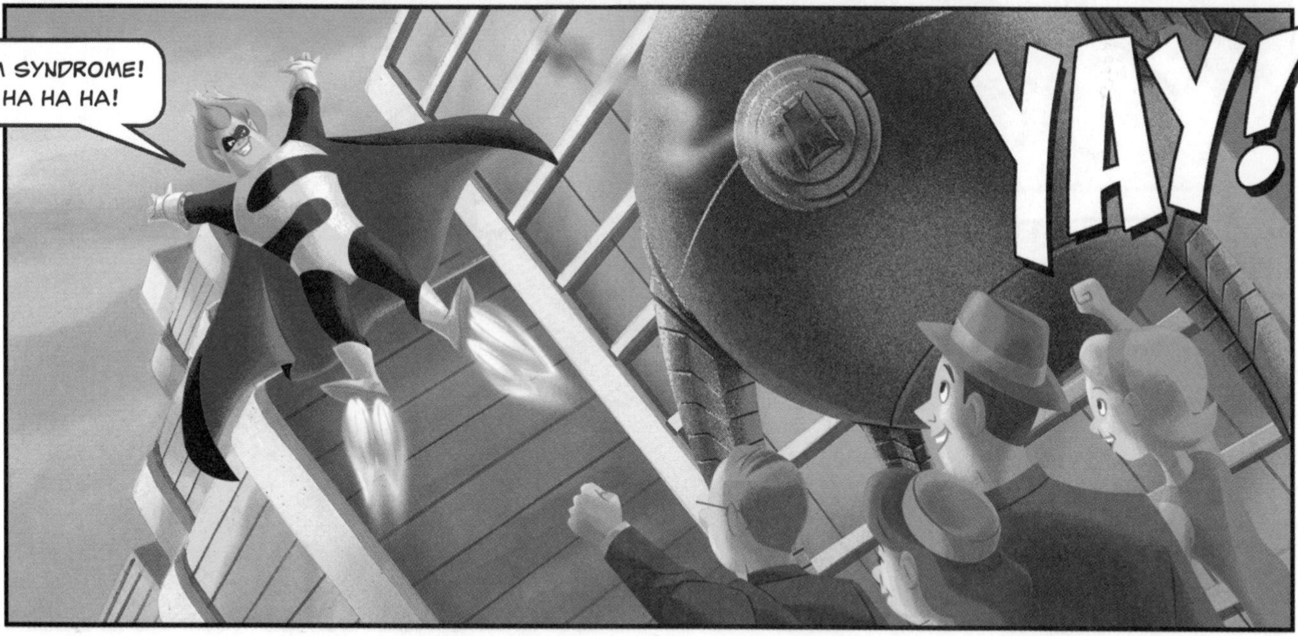
I'M SYNDROME! HA HA HA!
YAY!

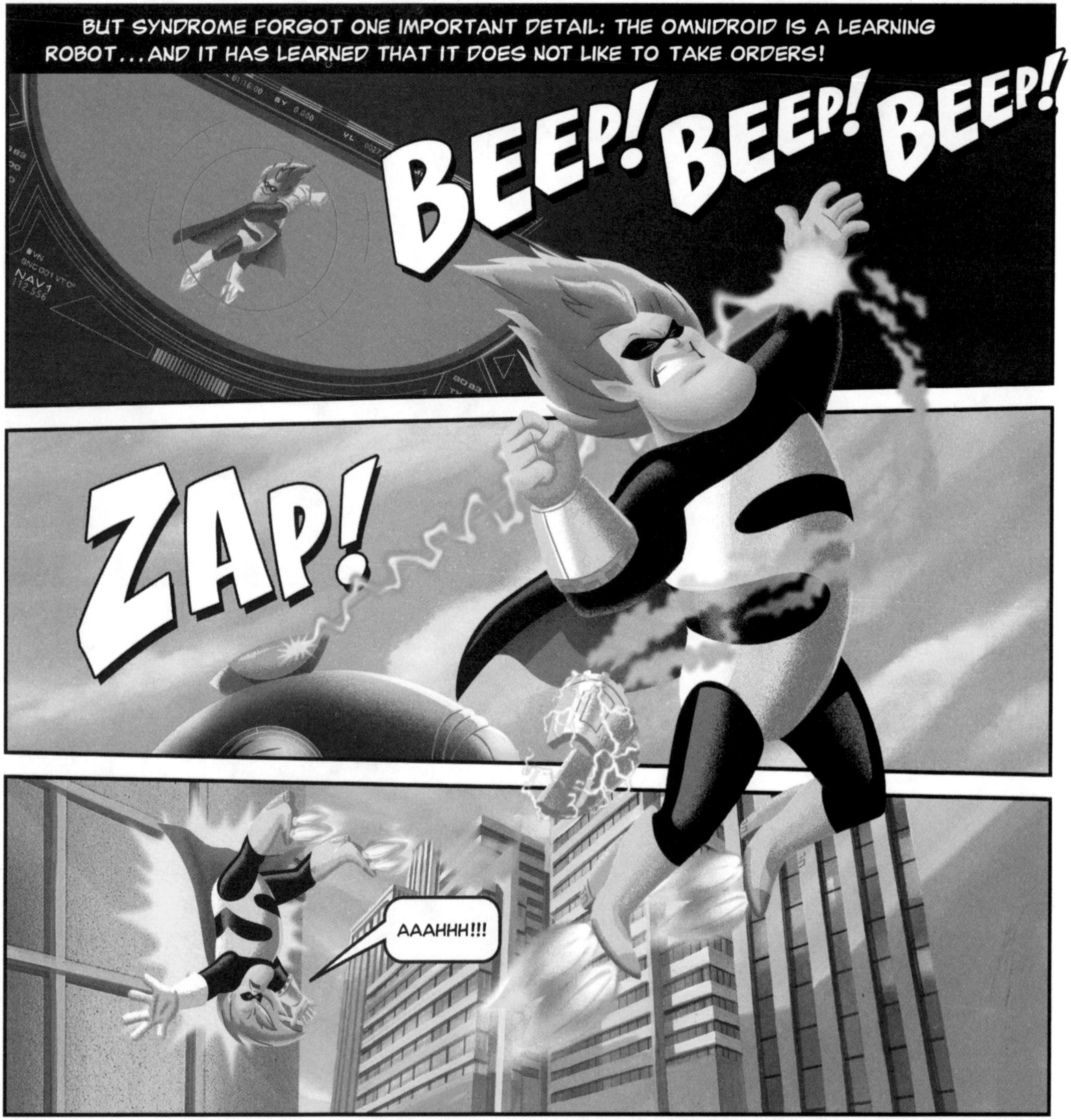
BUT SYNDROME FORGOT ONE IMPORTANT DETAIL: THE OMNIDROID IS A LEARNING ROBOT...AND IT HAS LEARNED THAT IT DOES NOT LIKE TO TAKE ORDERS!
BEEP! BEEP! BEEP!
ZAP!
AAAHHH!!!

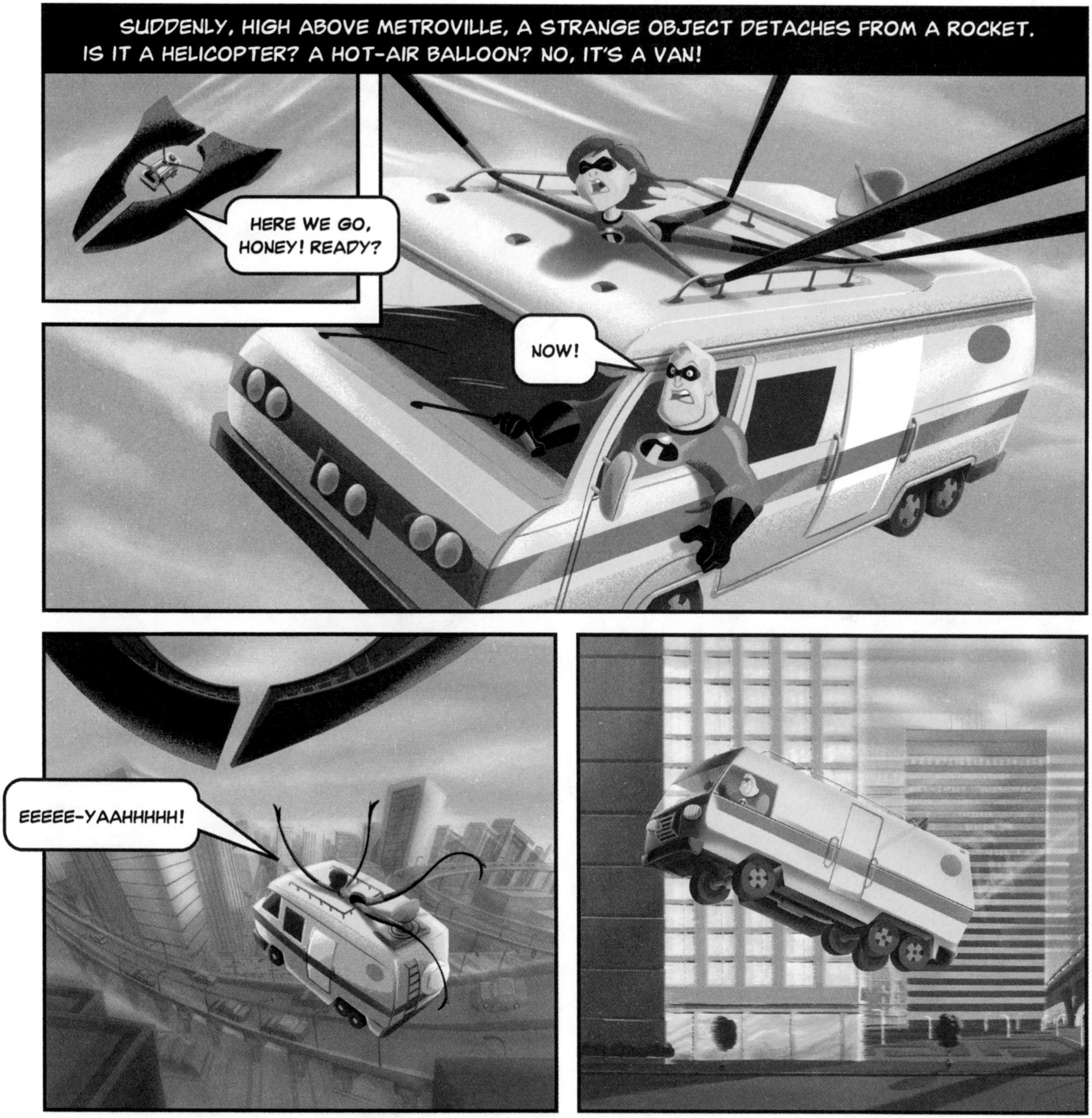
SUDDENLY, HIGH ABOVE METROVILLE, A STRANGE OBJECT DETACHES FROM A ROCKET. IS IT A HELICOPTER? A HOT-AIR BALLOON? NO, IT'S A VAN!
HERE WE GO, HONEY! READY?
NOW!
EEEEE-YAAHHHHH!

MR. INCREDIBLE SETS OUT TO BATTLE THE OMNIDROID...BUT WAIT! ELASTIGIRL STOPS HIM.

SO, TOGETHER AS A TEAM, THE INCREDIBLES PREPARE TO KICK SOME METAL.

I HAVE TO DO THIS ALONE.

WHILE I WATCH FROM THE SIDELINES?

I DON'T WANT TO LOSE YOU. I DON'T KNOW WHAT'LL HAPPEN.

HEY, WE'RE SUPERS. WHAT COULD HAPPEN?

VI, DASH! NO! LOOK OUT!

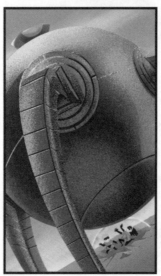

GO! GO!

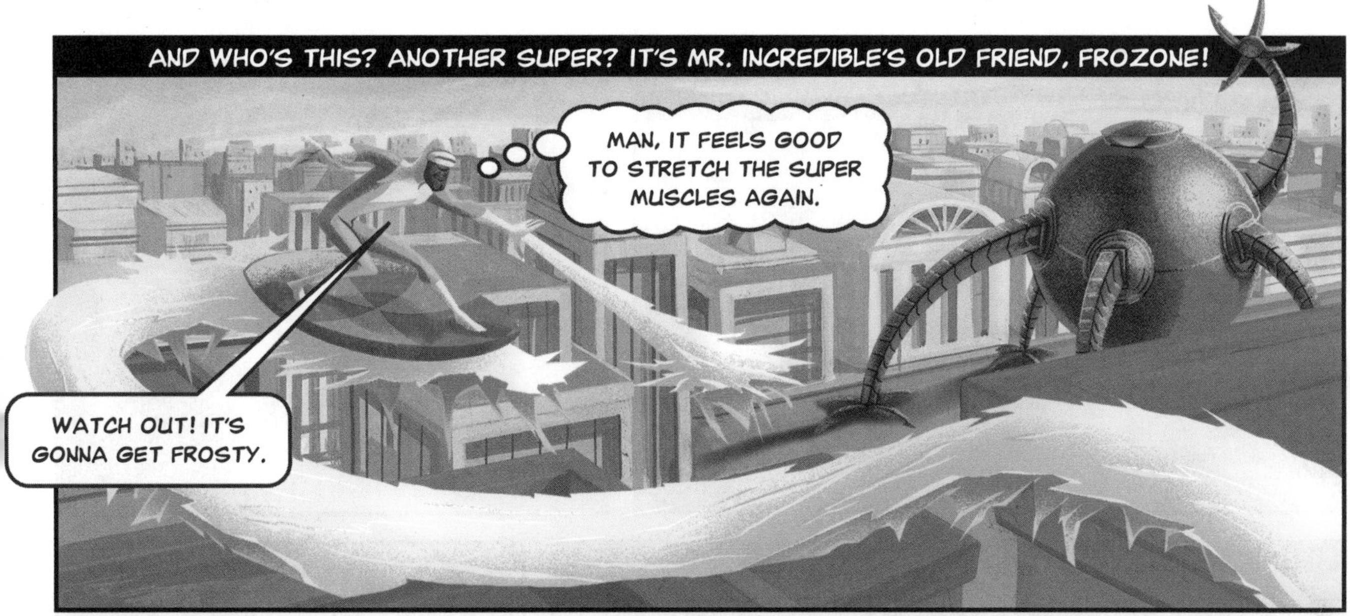
AND WHO'S THIS? ANOTHER SUPER? IT'S MR. INCREDIBLE'S OLD FRIEND, FROZONE!
MAN, IT FEELS GOOD TO STRETCH THE SUPER MUSCLES AGAIN.
WATCH OUT! IT'S GONNA GET FROSTY.

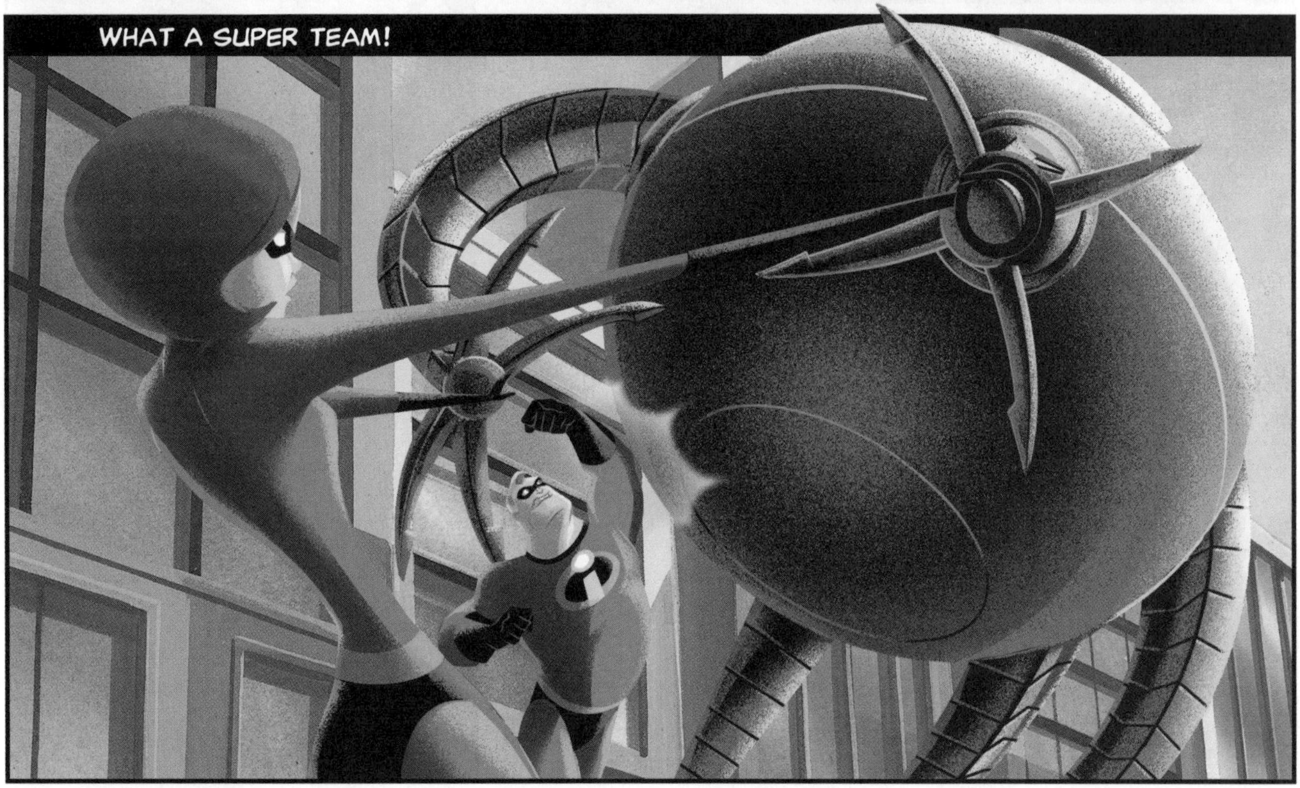
WHAT A SUPER TEAM!

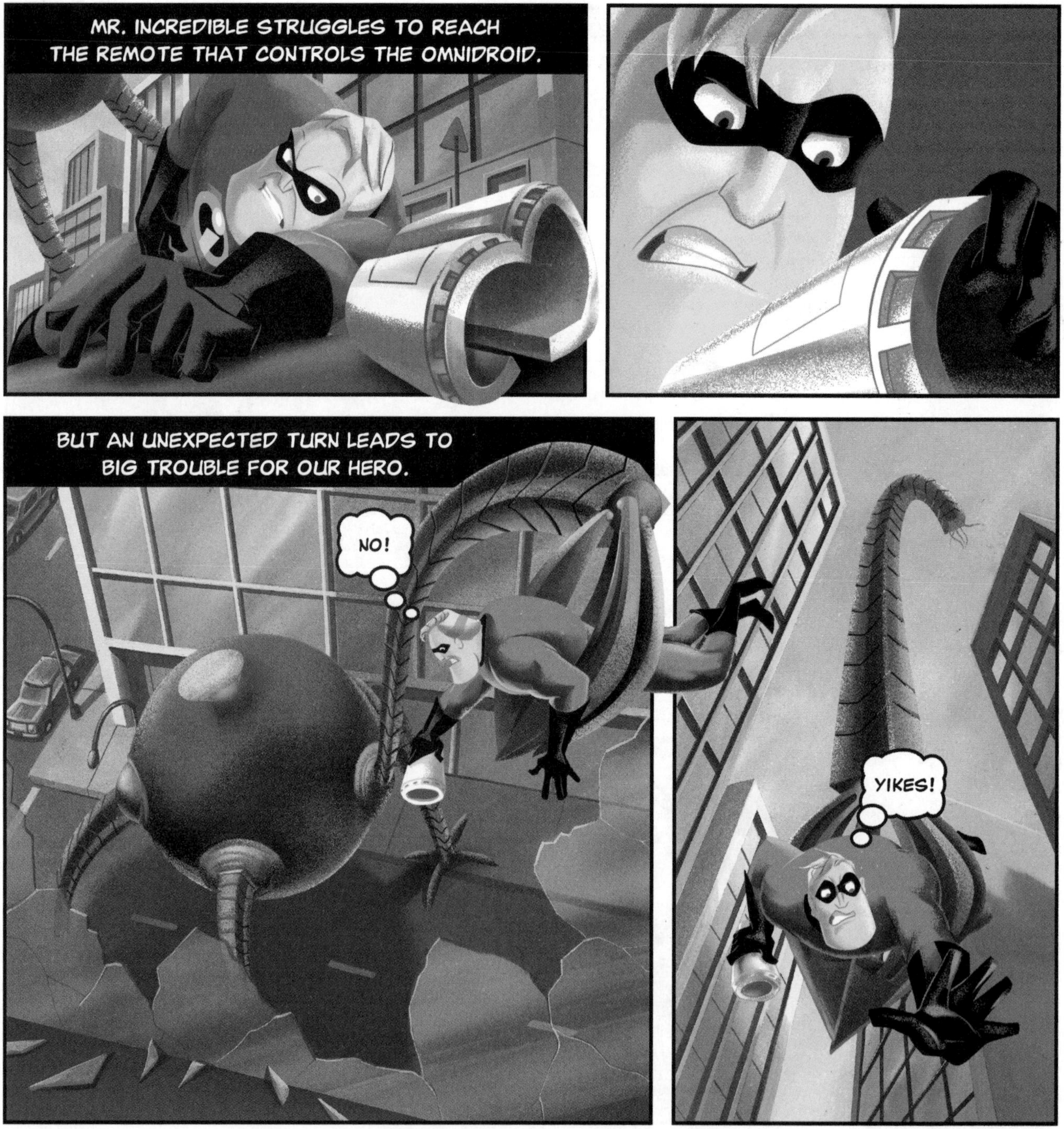
MR. INCREDIBLE STRUGGLES TO REACH
THE REMOTE THAT CONTROLS THE OMNIDROID.
BUT AN UNEXPECTED TURN LEADS TO
BIG TROUBLE FOR OUR HERO.
NO!
YIKES!

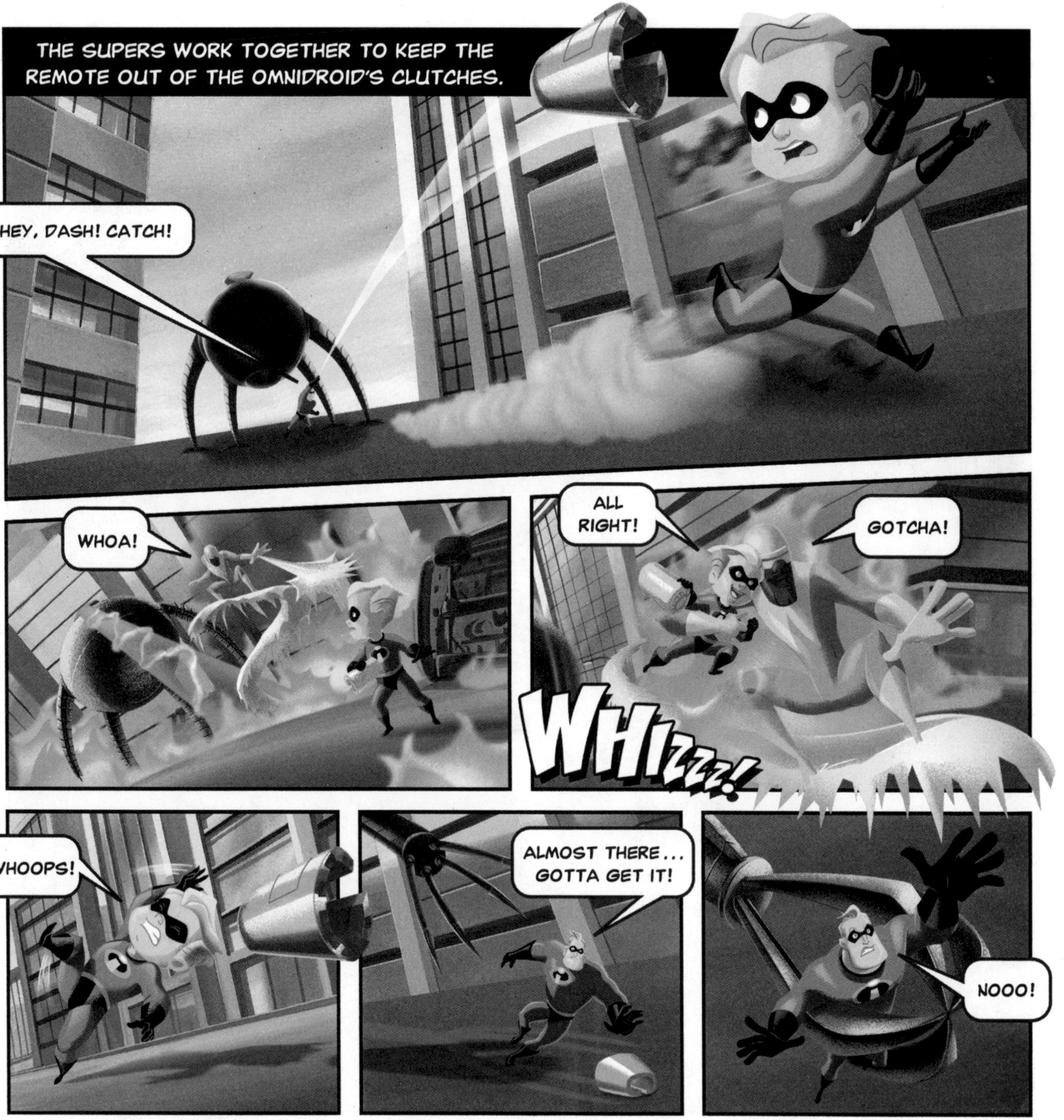
THE SUPERS WORK TOGETHER TO KEEP THE REMOTE OUT OF THE OMNIDROID'S CLUTCHES.
HEY, DASH! CATCH!
WHOA!
ALL RIGHT!
GOTCHA!
WHIZZZ!
WHOOPS!
ALMOST THERE . . . GOTTA GET IT!
NOOO!

FROZONE GIVES THE OMNIDROID THE COLD SHOULDER...

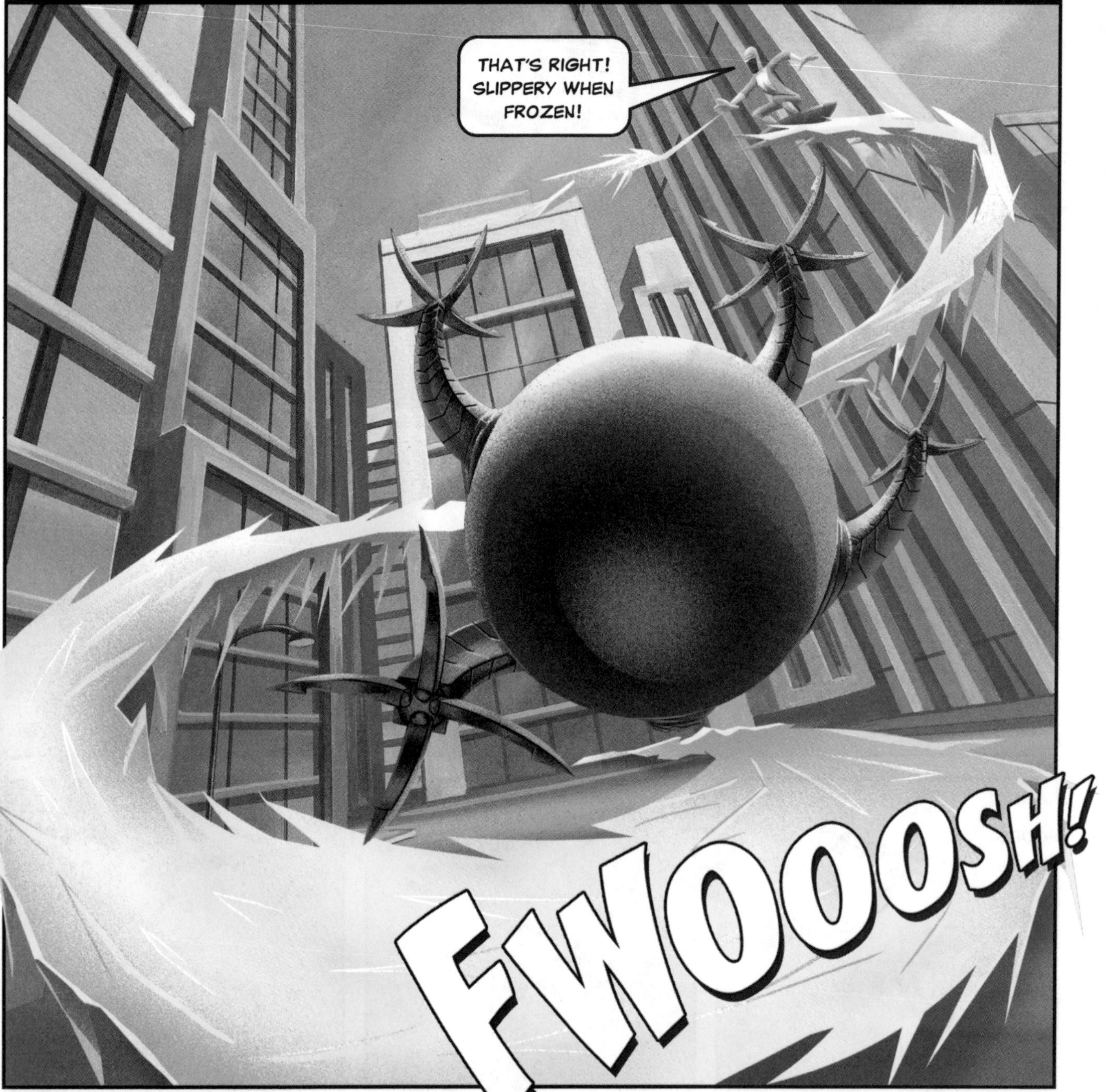
THAT'S RIGHT! SLIPPERY WHEN FROZEN!
FWOOOSH!

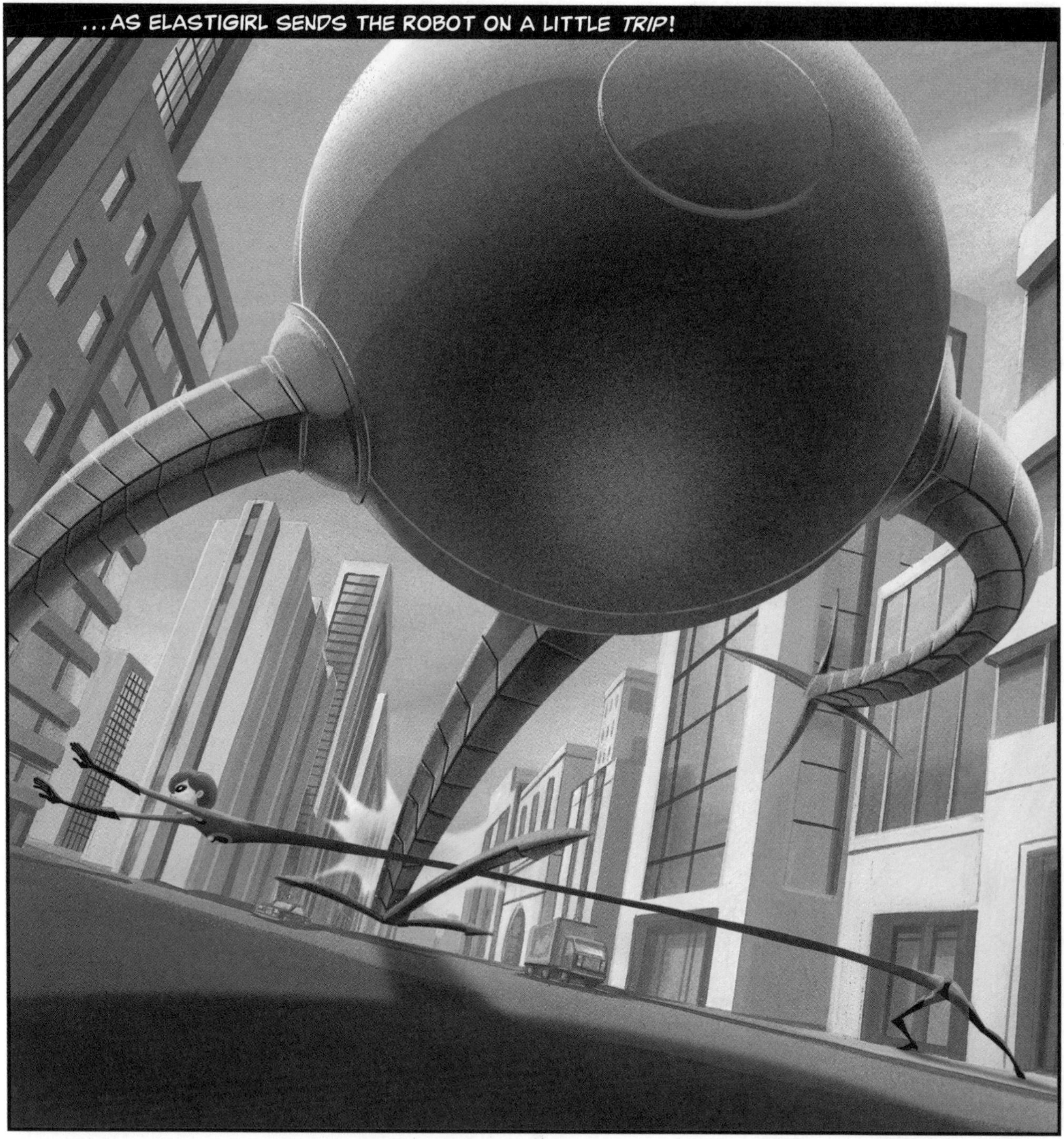
...AS ELASTIGIRL SENDS THE ROBOT ON A LITTLE *TRIP*!

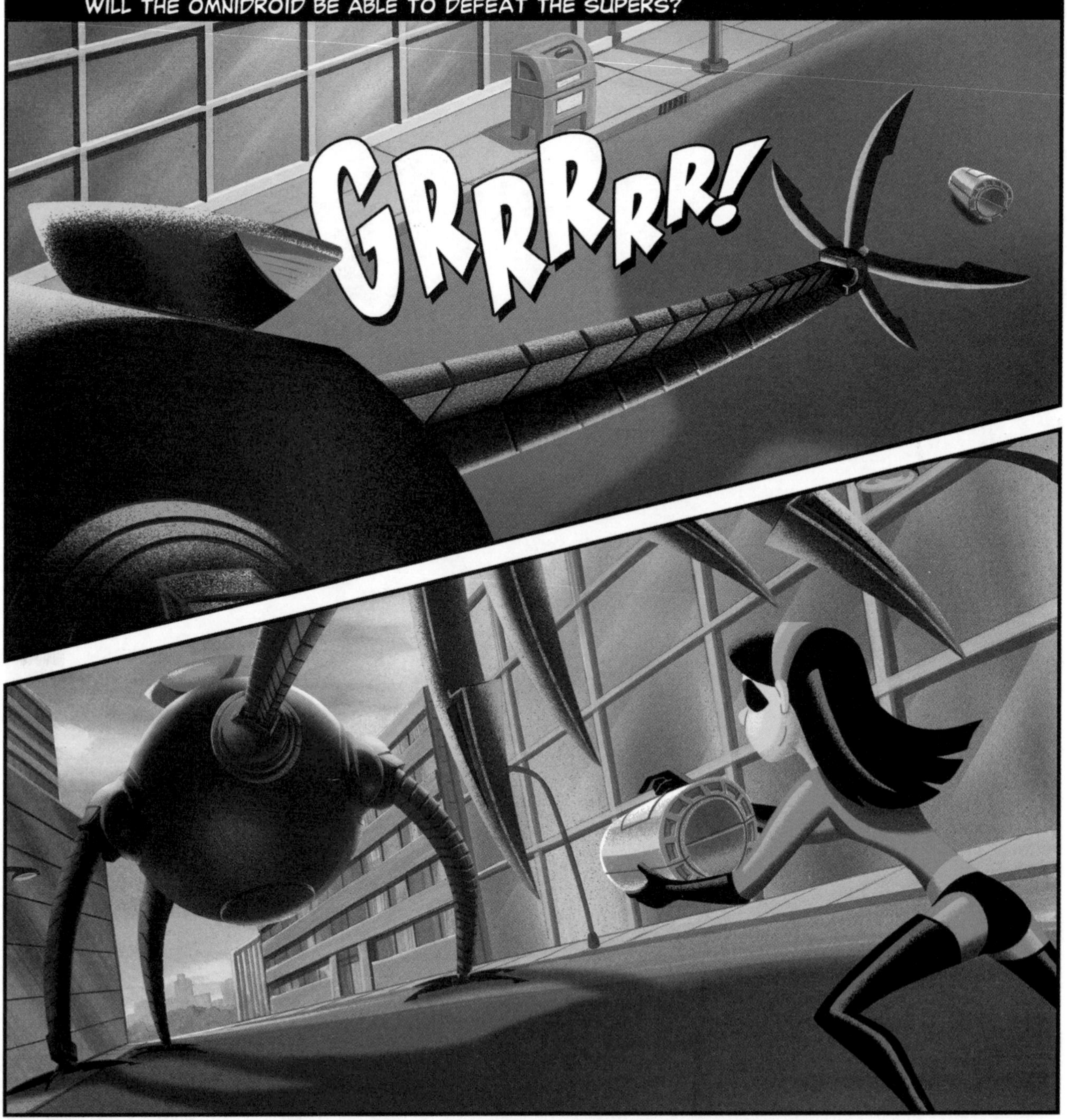
WILL THE OMNIDROID BE ABLE TO DEFEAT THE SUPERS?
GRRRRR!

NOT IF VIOLET CAN HELP IT!

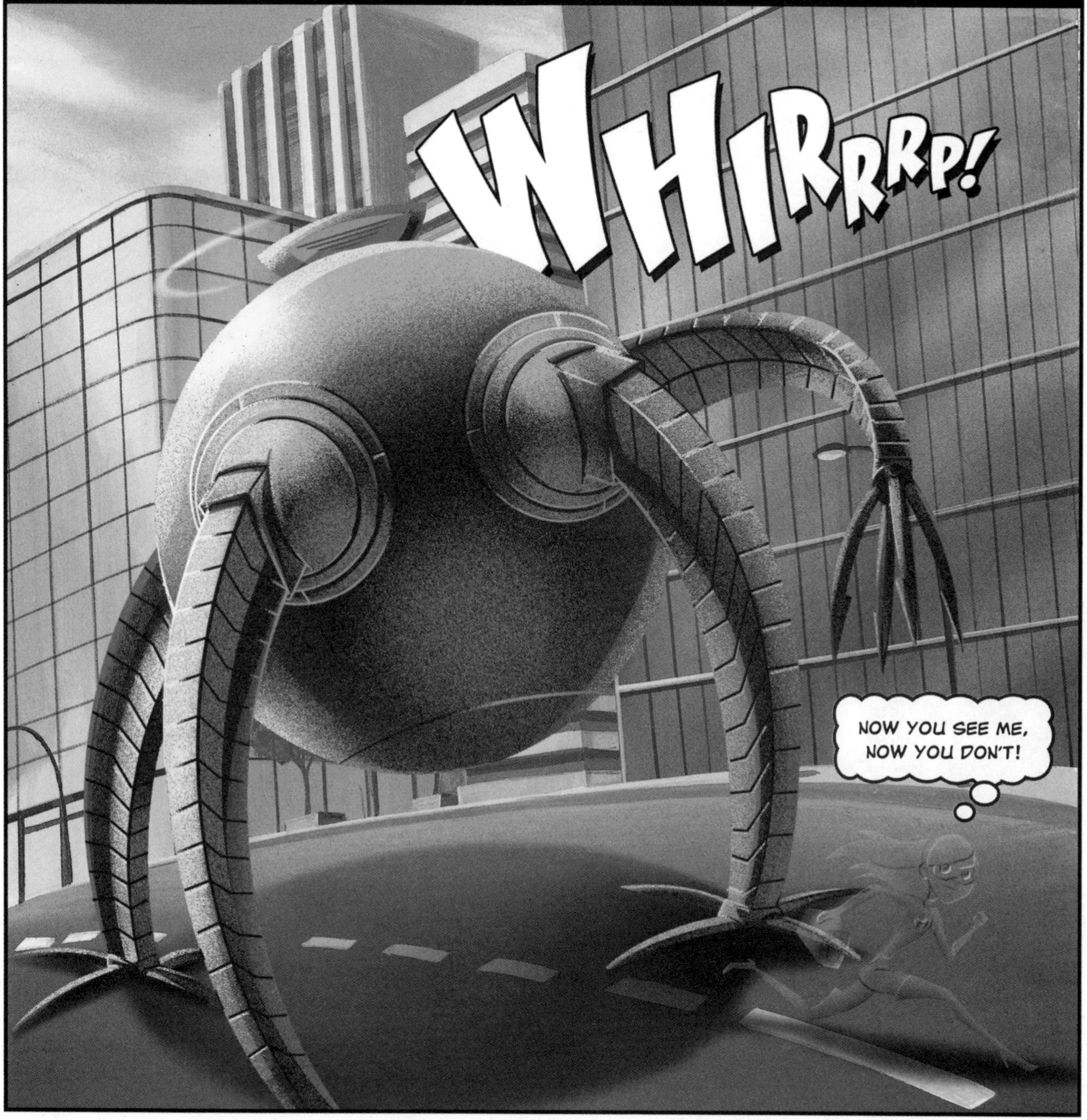
WHIRRRP!
NOW YOU SEE ME, NOW YOU DON'T!

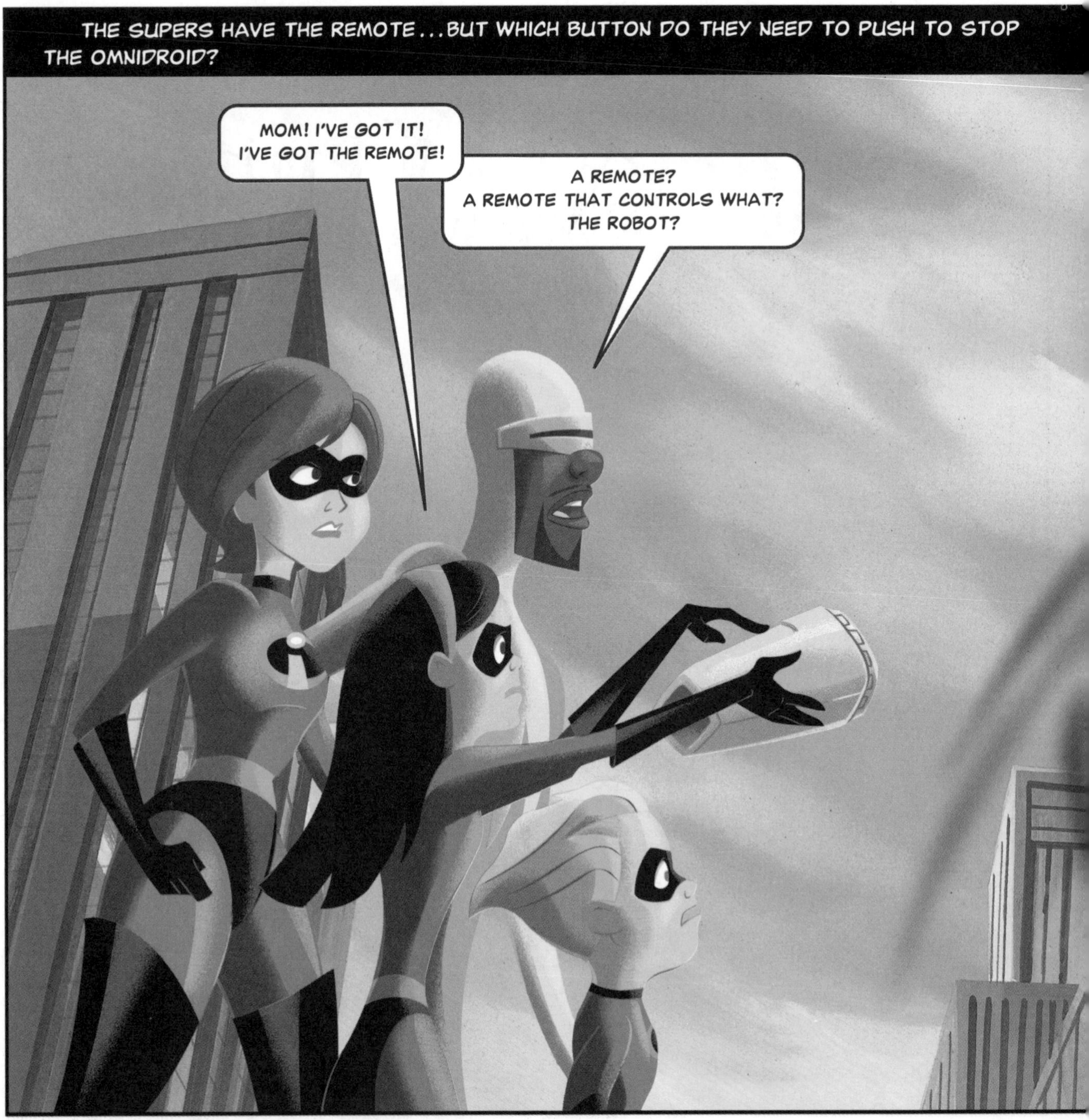
THE SUPERS HAVE THE REMOTE...BUT WHICH BUTTON DO THEY NEED TO PUSH TO STOP THE OMNIDROID?
MOM! I'VE GOT IT! I'VE GOT THE REMOTE!
A REMOTE? A REMOTE THAT CONTROLS WHAT? THE ROBOT?

FRANTICALLY TRYING TO DESTROY THE ROBOTIC MONSTER, OUR HEROES RAPIDLY PUSH BUTTONS ON THE REMOTE.

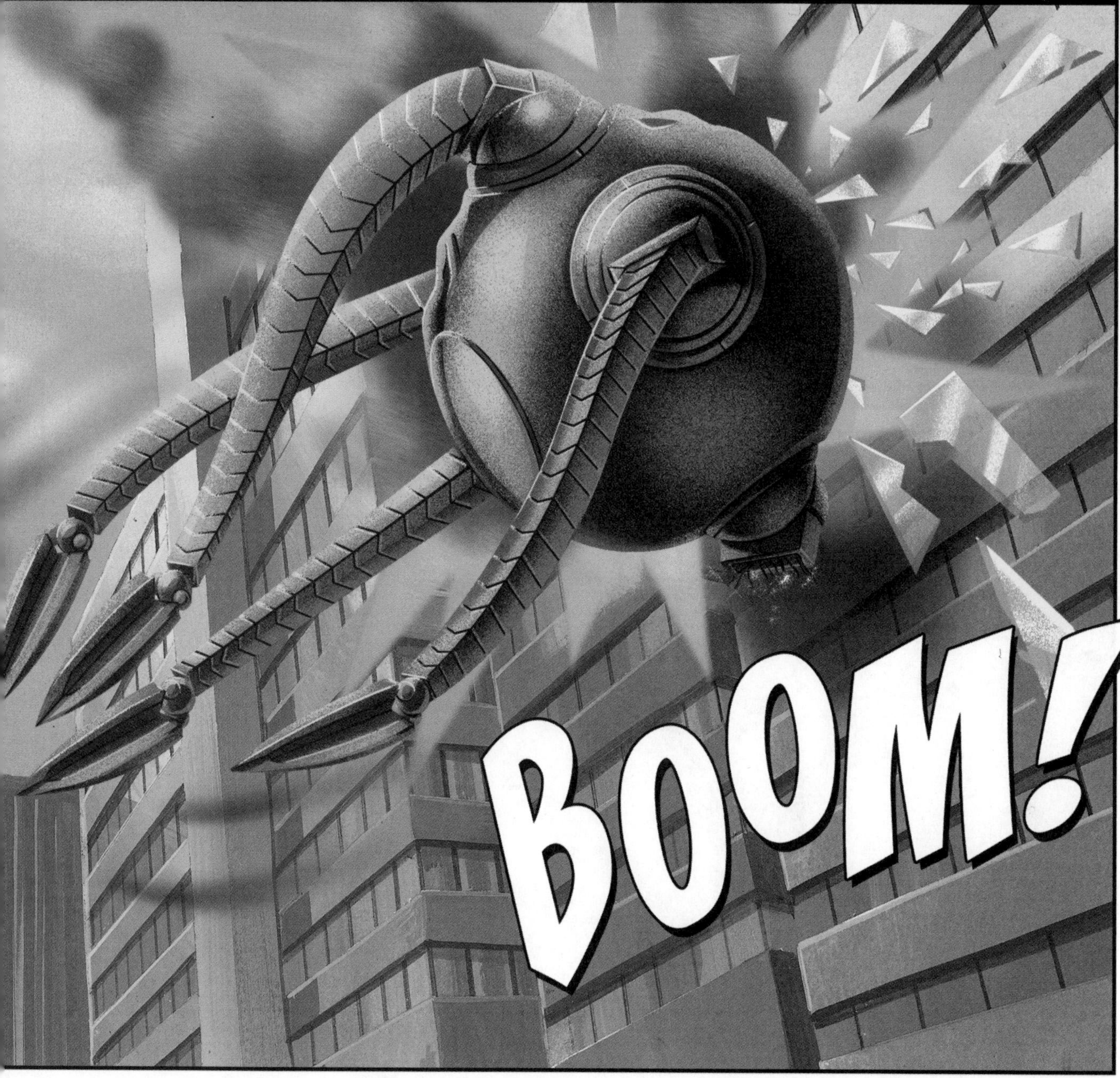
BOOM!

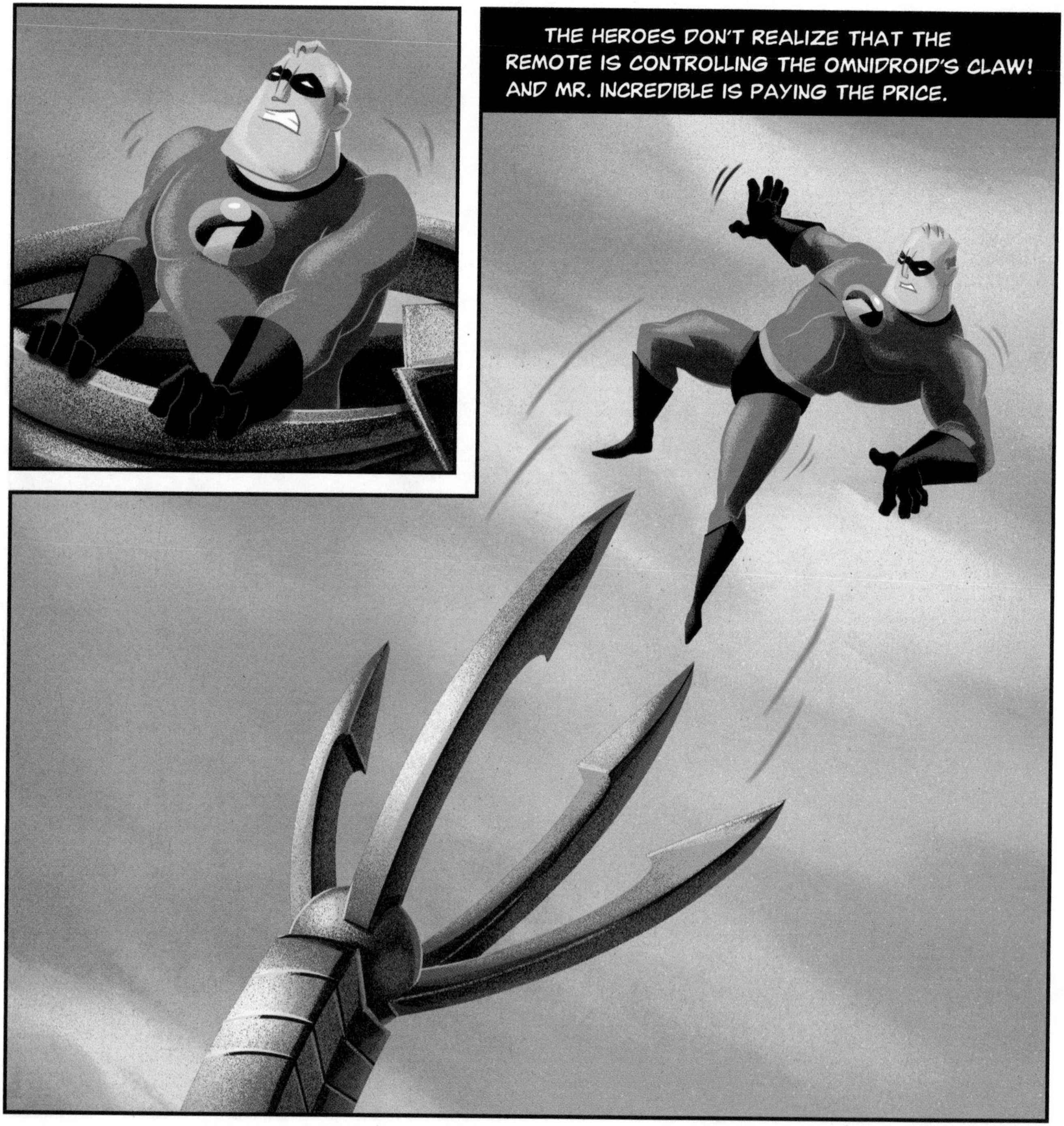
THE HEROES DON'T REALIZE THAT THE REMOTE IS CONTROLLING THE OMNIDROID'S CLAW! AND MR. INCREDIBLE IS PAYING THE PRICE.

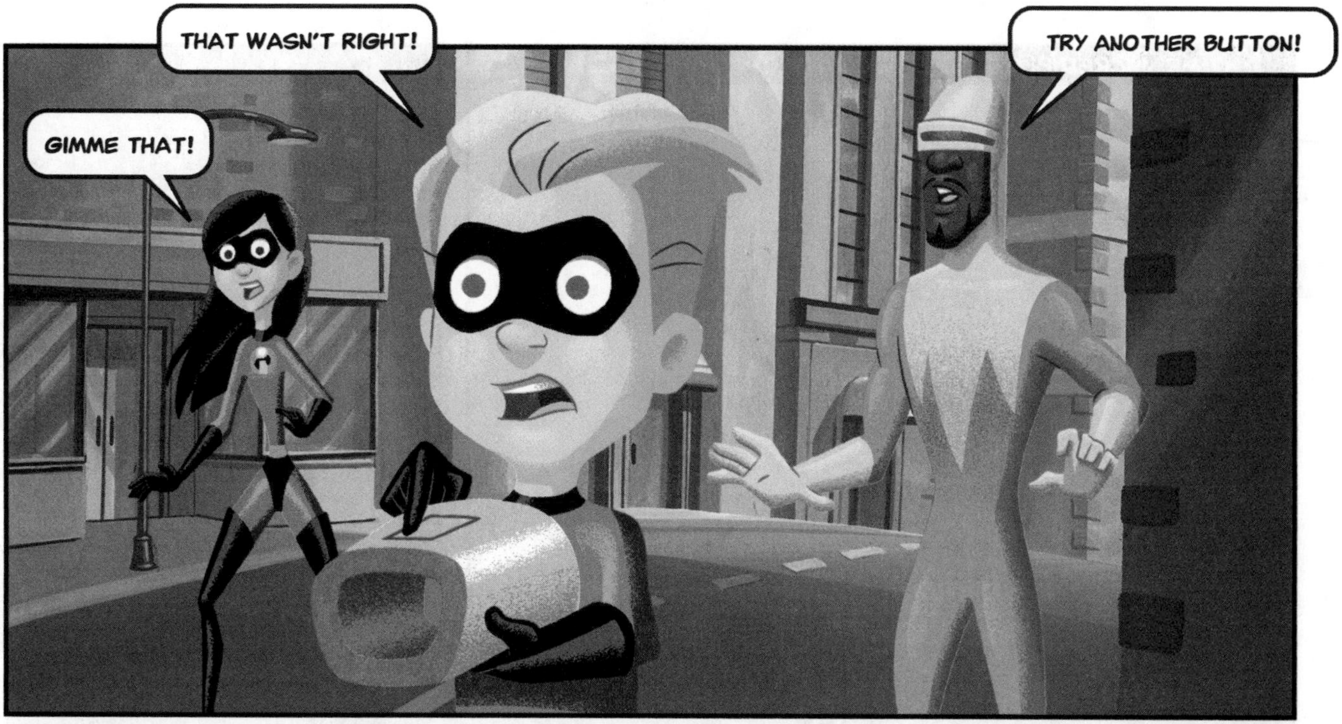
GIMME THAT!
THAT WASN'T RIGHT!
TRY ANOTHER BUTTON!

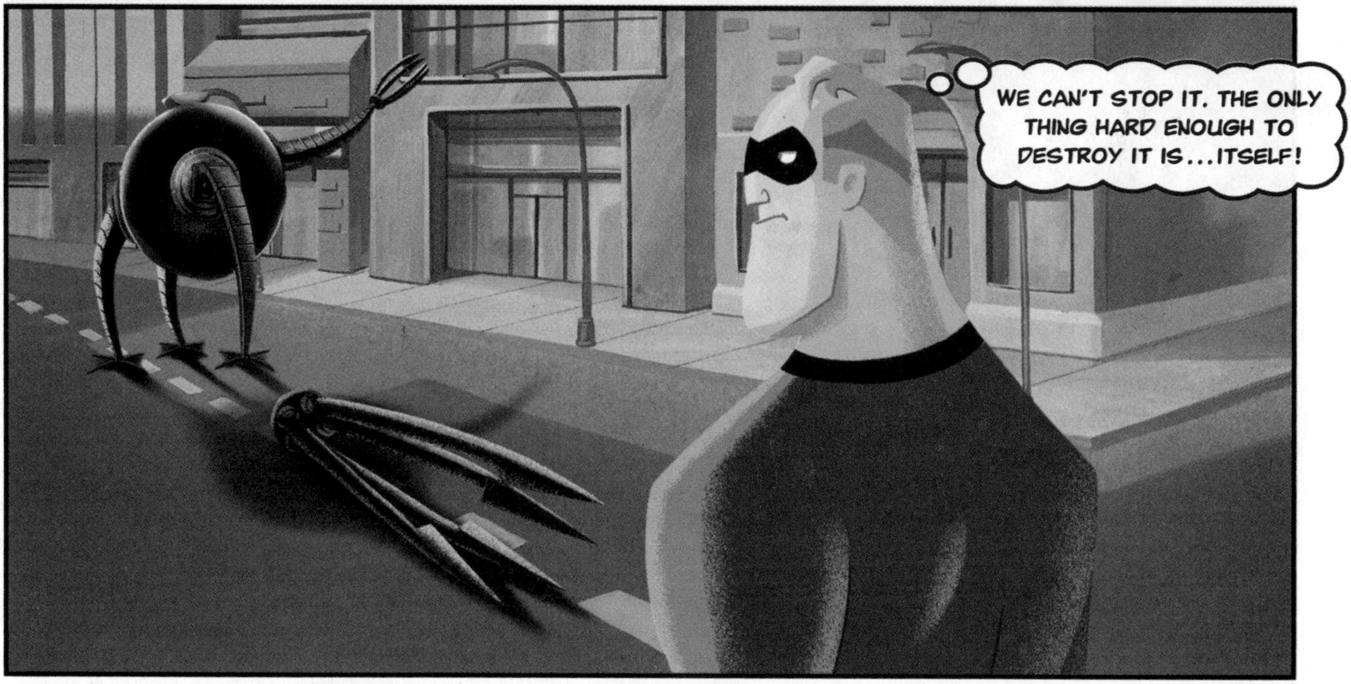
WE CAN'T STOP IT. THE ONLY THING HARD ENOUGH TO DESTROY IT IS...ITSELF!

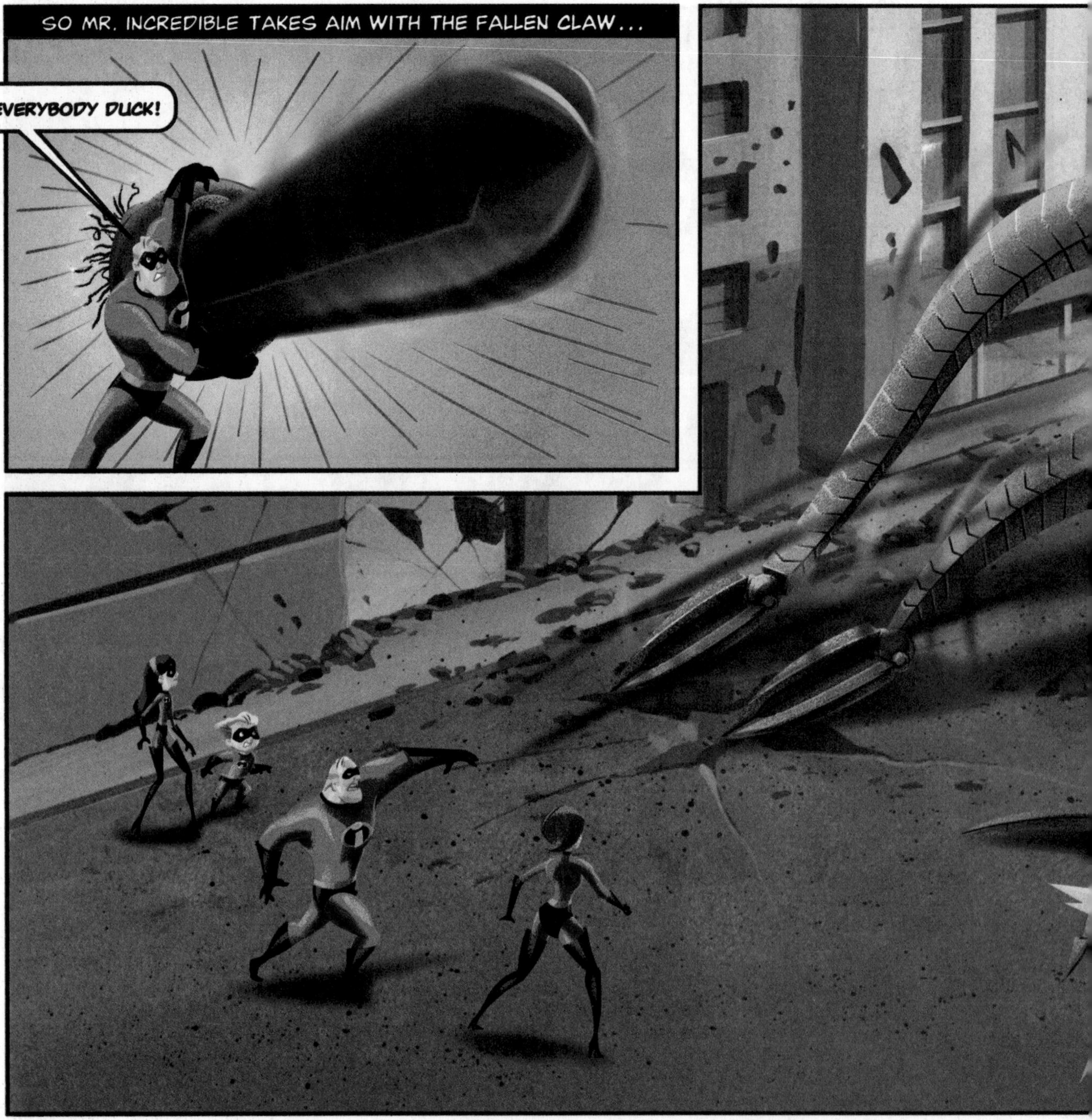
SO MR. INCREDIBLE TAKES AIM WITH THE FALLEN CLAW...
EVERYBODY DUCK!

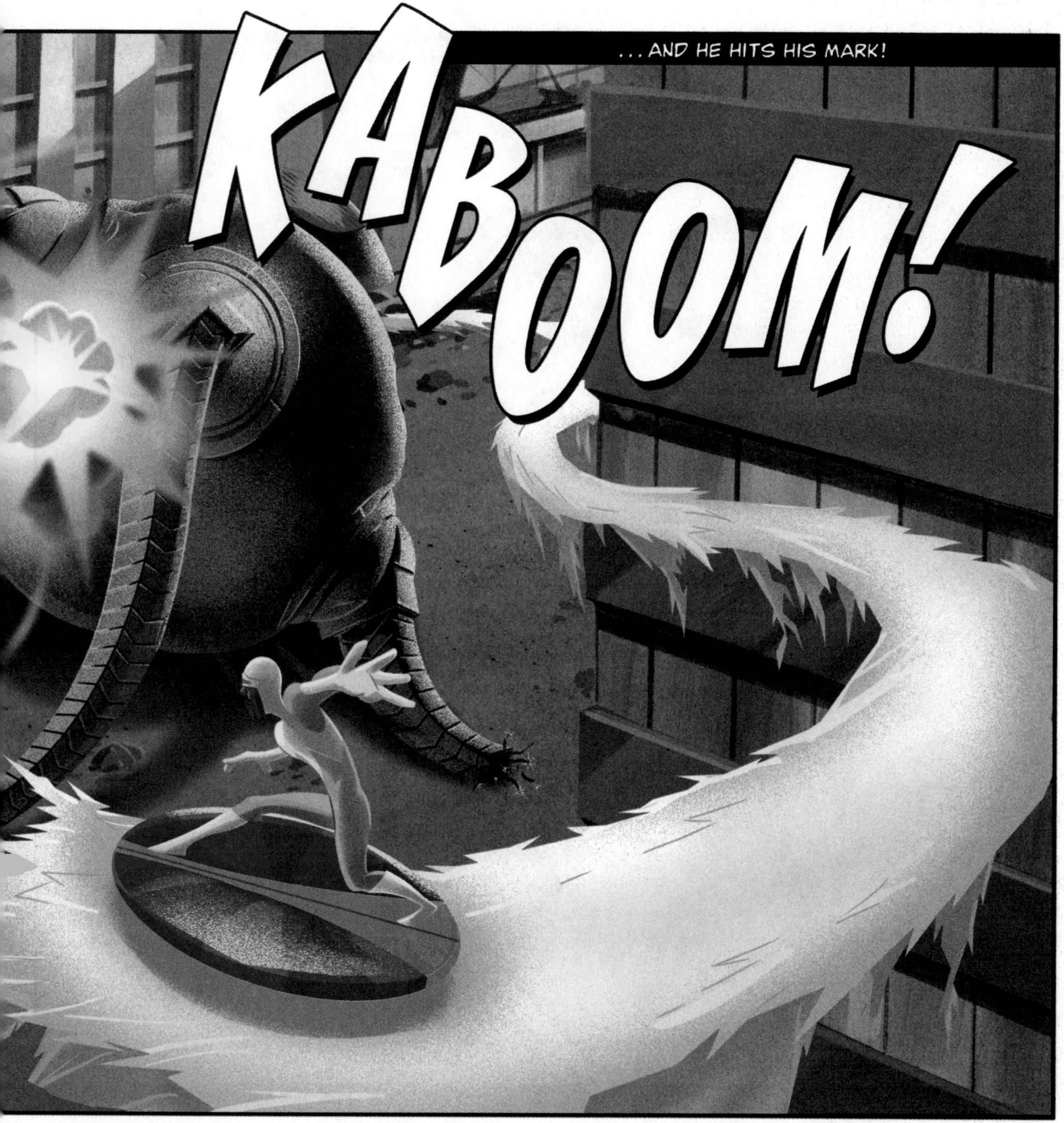

. . . AND HE HITS HIS MARK!
KABOOM!

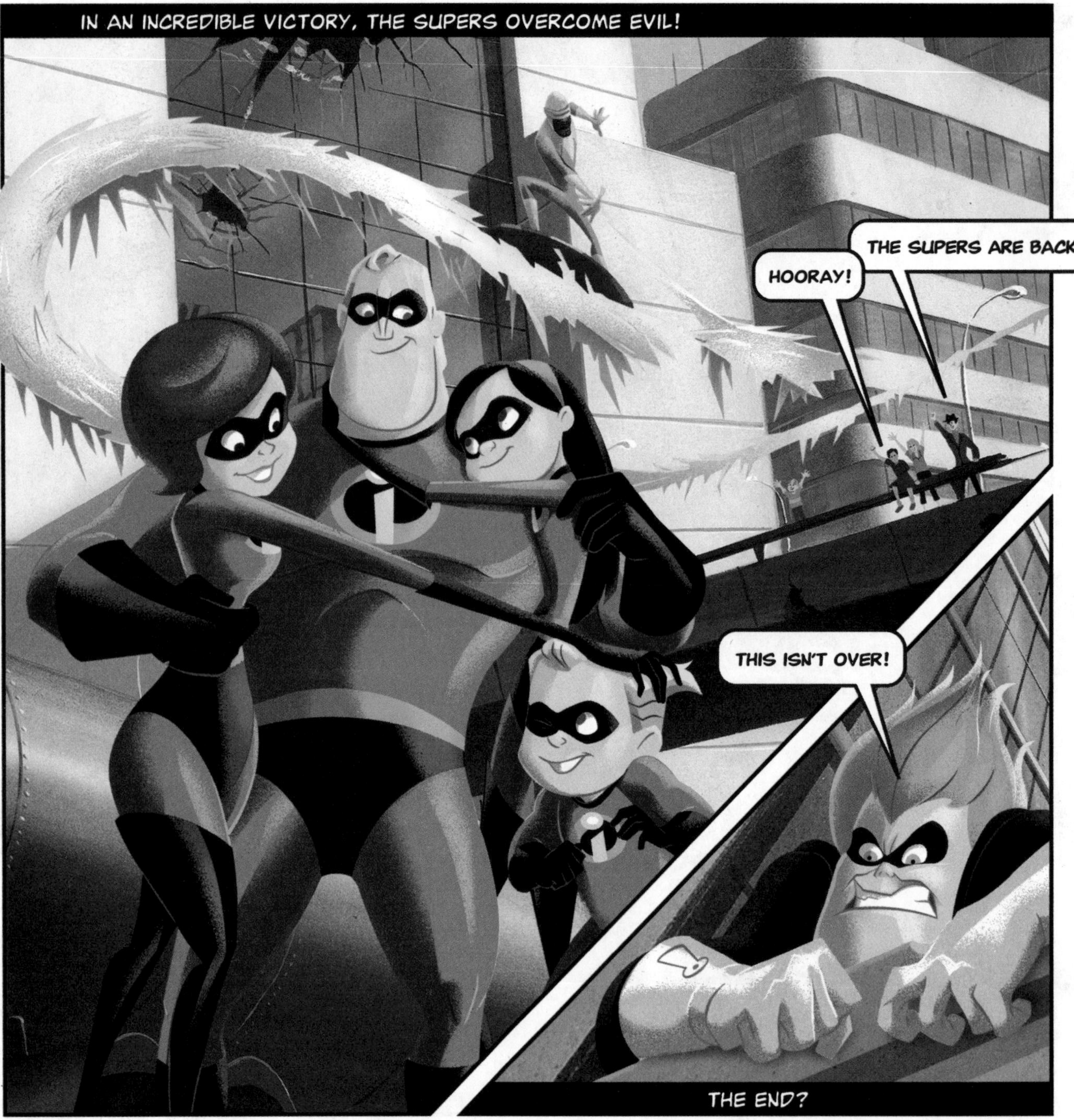
IN AN INCREDIBLE VICTORY, THE SUPERS OVERCOME EVIL!
HOORAY!
THE SUPERS ARE BACK!
THIS ISN'T OVER!
THE END?